THE GLITTER DRAGONS

DRAGON GIRLS

Azmina the Gold
Glitter Dragon

Maddy Mara

Azmina the Gold Glitter Dragon

by Maddy Mara

Scholastic Inc.

Copyright © 2021 by Maddy Mara
Illustrations by Thais Damião, copyright © 2021 by Scholastic Inc.

All rights reserved. Published by Scholastic Inc., *Publishers since 1920.* SCHOLASTIC and associated logos are trademarks and/or registered trademarks of Scholastic Inc.

The publisher does not have any control over and does not assume any responsibility for author or third-party websites or their content.

No part of this publication may be reproduced, stored in a retrieval system, or transmitted in any form or by any means, electronic, mechanical, photocopying, recording, or otherwise, without written permission of the publisher. For information regarding permission, write to Scholastic Inc., Attention: Permissions Department, 557 Broadway, New York, NY 10012.

This book is a work of fiction. Names, characters, places, and incidents are either the product of the author's imagination or are used fictitiously, and any resemblance to actual persons, living or dead, business establishments, events, or locales is entirely coincidental.

ISBN 978-1-338-68063-8

14 13   23 24 25

Printed in the U.S.A. 40

First printing 2021

Book design by Stephanie Yang

For Madeleine and Asmara

Azmina lay on her stomach in her brand-new backyard. The weather was warm for fall, but Azmina didn't feel the sun on her skin. She didn't notice a dog barking nearby. She didn't even hear her mom singing as she unpacked boxes in the house they had just moved into.

A strange sound had caught Azmina's

attention. The sound blocked out everything else. It was as if someone was whispering the first line of a song.

Magic Forest, Magic Forest, come explore...

Through a gap in the back fence, Azmina could see the edge of a forest. Was the music coming from there?

Azmina wasn't used to lying around on the grass, admiring trees. She thought of herself as a city girl, through and through. Well, she used to, anyway. She wasn't quite sure who she was in this new place yet. Back in the city she was always on the go: Singing lessons, playing soccer with her friends, organizing sleepovers.

But now, there wasn't anyone to organize sleepovers with. Everything had changed when she and her mom moved. Azmina liked the kids at her new school, but she  didn't have any besties yet.

In school, she had been assigned to a table with two other girls named Willa and Naomi. Somehow Azmina just knew that she was meant to be friends with them. She could feel it, fizzing like bubbles in a soft drink, deep in her stomach. But she wasn't quite sure how to make it happen.

Azmina sighed. She knew that friendships took time, but she hated being the new girl.

Magic Forest, Magic Forest, come explore...

Azmina sat up. The singing was clearer now. It was definitely coming from the forest! But it was different from any music Azmina had heard before. The melody was like the songs of a thousand birds and the babble of a river all mixed together with the rustling of leaves.

Azmina jumped up and ran to the back fence. She leaned over to get a closer look. Because she was from the city, she'd never seen a real forest up close before. She couldn't take her eyes off it! The leaves had turned the colors of fall. These were Azmina's favorites— brilliant red, fiery orange, and best of all, bright yellow. The forest floor looked like it was covered with treasure.

There was one tree that caught Azmina's attention. It was the tallest of all, with long and graceful branches. The tree's leaves shone as if they were made of pure gold. Azmina felt a little shiver of excitement run up her back.

There was something special about that tree. Something magical.

As she gazed into the forest, Azmina realized there were other curious things about it.

"I can smell flowers," Azmina muttered to herself. "But that doesn't make sense! Most of the flowers are gone now that it's fall."

But that wasn't even the strangest thing. Azmina thought she could smell pineapples and mangoes. Azmina didn't know much about forests, but she was pretty sure pineapples and mangoes didn't grow around here!

Now that she was closer, Azmina could hear more singing coming from the forest.

Magic Forest, Magic Forest, come explore.

Magic Forest, Magic Forest, hear my roar!

Hear my roar? What could that mean?

Azmina repeated the words out loud, softly at first: "Magic Forest, Magic Forest." But each time she said them, her voice got louder. One of the golden leaves on the tallest tree spun up into the air. It danced through the sky, swishing this way and that, leaving a glowing trail behind it.

Azmina watched as the leaf looped its way closer. When the leaf was above her, she leapt up and grabbed it. It was warm from the sunlight. Azmina's fingertips tingled.

Suddenly, she knew just what to do. Her voice rang out strong and true as she began to sing:

Magic Forest, Magic Forest, come explore.

Magic Forest, Magic Forest, hear my roar!

Instantly, a hot gust of wind swirled around her. Azmina closed her eyes as she was whooshed up into the air, spun around, and then dropped down onto the ground again. It took only a few seconds, but Azmina knew something amazing had happened. Something life-changing.

2

Azmina opened her eyes to see that she was no longer in her backyard. Instead, she was standing in the middle of the forest. Up close, it was even more beautiful than it had seemed from her yard. Vines twisted around tree trunks, heavy with fruits Azmina had never seen before. Flowers of every possible color covered the ground like a carpet. Birdsong filled the air around her.

Azmina noticed a tiny, fuzzy pink ball attached to a nearby vine. As she watched, the ball began to grow—right before her eyes! Within seconds, a perfect, ripe fruit had formed. It looked like a peach but smelled like raspberries. Azmina couldn't resist picking it and taking a bite. To her surprise, it tasted exactly like chocolate!

What was this place?

The tropical smells tickled her nose, and soon Azmina felt a sneeze building up. Azmina opened her mouth, threw back her head, and ... *ACHOO!* She just loved sneezing!

It always felt like scratching a trouble-some itch.

Golden sparks fluttered down around Azmina. She looked at the glittering mist in surprise. Had she done that with her sneeze?

Azmina's heart pounded wildly. Something amazing was going on. But what, exactly?

Through the trees, Azmina spotted a shimmering lake. Azmina decided to check it out, and started to jog toward it. She had always been a fast runner, but today her legs felt stronger and faster than ever before. Soon, she was sprinting through the trees at top speed. She reached the lakeshore in no time.

Skidding to a stop at the lake's edge, Azmina peered in. What she saw in the water made her gasp. Staring back at her from the watery surface was some kind of magnificent creature.

Azmina leapt away from the lake. She

whipped around to face whatever it was that was standing behind her. But she was all alone. She looked from left to right. Nothing. Maybe the creature was under the water? Or maybe she'd imagined the whole thing? Azmina crept back to the lake and looked in once more.

There it was again! It was covered in golden scales that sent tiny circles of light across the water's surface. Two elegant golden ears twitched on top of its head. Around its eyes were swirling patterns.

It was a dragon!

"Um…hello?" said Azmina, because she wasn't quite sure what to say to a dragon. As

she spoke, Azmina saw the dragon's mouth move at the same time.

Azmina stared at the dragon, her thoughts whirling. She moved her head, and the dragon's head moved, too. She stuck out her tongue, AND SO DID THE DRAGON!

Azmina looked down at her feet...except

she didn't have feet anymore. She had big golden paws and powerful golden legs.

In surprise, Azmina stepped backward and promptly fell over. She turned to see what she had tripped on and spotted an enormous golden snake, gleaming in the sun.

"Ahh!" she cried in alarm, scrambling to get away from the snake.

But the snake followed her!

That was when Azmina realized it wasn't a snake at all. It was a tail. But was it attached to her? Azmina tried to twitch it. Yes! The tail swished through the air in a satisfying way, leaving a ribbon of glitter that sparkled for a moment, then faded away.

Just then, a roar came from over near the bushes. Without thinking, Azmina threw open her mouth and roared back. She was so loud, the trees swayed! And once again, specks of glitter swirled in the air.

Azmina looked over at the bushes. What had roared at her? Something peeked its head out from behind a fern. Was it a tiny lion cub? Or a baby leopard? The cub had soft golden fur like a lion, but was also dotted all over with spots. And these weren't just any regular spots. They were neon yellow!

"Hello there, you little cutie!" said Azmina. She tried to whisper, but it turns out it's hard to speak softly when you are a dragon!

The cub didn't seem scared. He bounded toward Azmina like a puppy. As he got closer, Azmina saw he had beautiful wings, patterned like a butterfly's.

Azmina chuckled as the strange little creature nuzzled into her leg. She reached down to pat him, but with a powerful flap of his wings, the cub lifted into the air. He hovered just above Azmina's head, doing midair somersaults with a cheerful look on his face.

"Hey, come back, you little butterfly-cub

thingy!" cooed Azmina. "I wonder what I should call you. How about Buttercub? Like buttercup, but with a *B* at the end?"

Buttercub gave a rumbly purr and flew over to press his cheek against Azmina's. His little whiskers were tickly.

Azmina laughed. "I'll take that as a yes!"

As Azmina reached up to give Buttercub a pat, she felt herself lift off the ground. A whooshing sound filled the air. Her stomach lurched, like she was in a very fast elevator or on a roller coaster.

Excitement thumped in Azmina's chest. She knew what was happening. Sure enough, when she looked over her shoulder, she saw two huge, gorgeous wings sticking out from her back. They looked like they were made of pure gold, and were etched with delicate patterns. Each time she flapped her wings, she sent glowing, glittering dust into the air.

Azmina grinned with delight. She was flying! She couldn't believe this was happening. Her favorite dreams had always been about flying. And every birthday, when she blew out the candles on her cake, her wish never changed: *I wish I could fly . . .*

Buttercub butted her chest with his head, then flew a little way off.

"Want me to follow you?" asked Azmina, hovering on the spot.

The little animal nodded and let out a noise that sounded a lot like yes.

"Hang on, did you just speak?" cried Azmina.

"No," purred Buttercub. "You just imagined it."

"Wh-what?" stuttered Azmina. She was very confused.

But before she could ask anything else, the little cub whooshed off. He looked over his shoulder, checking to see if she was following.

"I'm coming!" called Azmina. "But I won't be as fast as you. I'm new to this flying business, remember."

With each beat of her wings, Azmina was getting better at flying. All the same, she stayed fairly close to the ground, just in case

she fell. Buttercub zoomed around her, twisting and looping.

"Quit showing off!" Azmina laughed. "I'll be as good as you with practice, just you wait."

It wasn't long before they came to a place where the trees grew too thickly to fly between.

Buttercub dropped softly to the ground and scampered over to a narrow gap in the thicket. Warm honey-colored light filtered through the space.

"Do we go through here?" asked Azmina, bumping down clumsily beside Buttercub. She was going to have to work on her takeoffs and landings!

"You must go on without me. But I'll see you again soon," Buttercub purred.

"Ha! You can speak!" exclaimed Azmina.

Buttercub gave a furry kind of laugh. "Of course I can. All animals in the Magic Forest talk, if you know how to listen."

"Really? That's so cool," breathed Azmina.

Somehow, this was almost as exciting as discovering she was a dragon.

Azmina felt sad to leave Buttercub, but she was very curious to see what lay beyond the trees. She gave him a thank-you scratch between his ears, took a deep breath, and squeezed through the gap. It was a tight fit and the branches scratched her, but Azmina pushed on. What would she find on the other side?

3

As Azmina pressed through the very last bush, she tripped on a tree root and fell flat on her face. If that weren't bad enough, she also gave a loud hiccup. Azmina often got the hiccups, but this was the first time she'd ever hiccuped out a little golden flame!

Letting out another fire hiccup, Azmina

picked herself up and looked around. There was something strange about the air. It was shimmering—like air does on a really, really hot day. But it felt lovely and cool under the trees.

Azmina reached out to touch the shimmering air—and her paw disappeared! Quickly, she jerked backward, and her paw reappeared.

Was this some sort of portal? Or maybe a force field? It was all very strange, but Azmina didn't feel afraid. Buttercub had led her here, and she trusted him.

Taking a deep breath, Azmina stepped into the twinkling air. She felt a slight whooshing sensation and found herself in a light-filled glade. Sweet-smelling grass was cloud soft beneath her paws. Bell-shaped flowers tinkled as they swayed in the breeze. Butterflies circled the air, humming delicate melodies as they flitted about.

In the middle of the glade stood a single tree. Its glossy branches were covered in rustling golden leaves. Azmina's heart skipped a beat. She was sure this was the beautiful tree she'd seen from her backyard!

Hovering in midair beside the tree was a gorgeous multicolored dragon. In shape and size it was similar to Azmina, but its markings were different. This dragon had bright purple scales and rainbow stripes covering its wings and body.

"Um . . . hi!" said Azmina. "I know I look like a dragon, but I'm actually a girl."

The rainbow dragon puffed multicolored glitter from her nostrils. "You must be a Dragon Girl, like me," said the dragon. She had a human-sounding voice, only much louder. She also sounded familiar. "You're Azmina, right?"

Azmina stared at her. "How did you know?" To herself, she thought: *What is a Dragon Girl?*

The rainbow dragon puffed more glitter into the air. "We were told you were coming. We wanted to tell you at school, but we promised to wait."

Azmina felt really confused now. "We? There's more of us?"

"Yes! The third one is—"

Before the rainbow dragon could finish, a whooshing sound filled the air, and another dragon pushed through the shimmering force field, snout first.

Azmina gave a little roar of surprise, flapping her wings. She rose up off the ground, did a wonky spin, and crash-landed. Butterflies scattered in all directions.

The new dragon was a dazzling silvery blue color with sparkling green eyes. She held out a paw to help Azmina up, laughing kindly. "Don't worry. When I flew for the first time yesterday I went splat into a tree." She turned to the rainbow dragon. "Heya, Naomi. You got here quickly!"

Azmina spun around to face the rainbow dragon. "Naomi? From school?"

"Got it in one!" The rainbow dragon smiled as the silver dragon laughed again. Azmina had heard that laugh before. "Willa!" she cried.

The silver dragon nodded, her eyes twinkling. "Yup, it's me! Wild, isn't it? I still can't quite believe it. And Naomi and I have had twenty-four hours to get used to the idea."

Azmina didn't usually struggle to find things to say. But right then, she was speechless.

"I know this is a lot to take in," said Naomi, as though she could read Azmina's mind. "But just go with it. There's going to be a lot more to find out today. Like, why we've been summoned here."

"We've been summoned?" asked Azmina. She thought back to the chant she'd heard in her backyard. It all made sense now. The forest had been calling to her!

"It's the only way into the Magic Forest," explained Willa. "Just like you can only enter this special glade if you have good intentions. The Tree Queen explained yesterday. If you were a baddie, that shimmering air would be as hard as concrete."

"Who's the Tree Queen?" asked Azmina.

Willa breathed out a puff of silvery smoke as she laughed. "You're about to find out. Tree Queen? We're all here!"

Azmina looked around. As far as she could see, there was no one else in the glade. But as she watched, the tall tree in the center began to sway back and forth. It almost looked like it was dancing.

Gradually, the lower part of the trunk became a flowing gown, moss green in color. The branches transformed into elegant arms. A face framed by long flowing hair became clear against the top of the trunk.

"Thank you for coming, Glitter Dragons," the

tree person said. Her voice was warm and firm. "And welcome, Azmina, the final member of the glitter group. I am the Tree Queen of the Magic Forest. I am the one who called you here today."

"We're Glitter Dragons?" Azmina grinned. That would explain the sparkles in the air every time she moved. Or sneezed, hiccuped, or roared!

The Tree Queen swayed and smiled. "Yes! Willa is the Silver Glitter Dragon, and Naomi is the Rainbow Glitter Dragon. And you, Azmina, are the Gold Glitter Dragon. You've joined us just in time. We need your help."

Azmina felt a shot of energy run through

her. She hoped that whatever help was needed, it would involve lots of flying.

"The Shadow Sprites have returned," said the Tree Queen. She suddenly sounded very serious.

"Shadow Sprites?" repeated Azmina. "Are they bad?"

"I am afraid so," said the Tree Queen grimly. "Long, long ago, the Magic Forest was ruled by a cruel and terrible queen. The Shadow Queen. The Shadow Sprites were her helpers. Back then, the forest was a wild and scary place. It took many, many years, but we finally defeated the Shadow Queen and her sprites. We thought they were banished for good. But they have been spotted again, here in the forest."

The Tree Queen let out a deep sigh. "I fear that the Shadow Sprites are planning to take control of the forest so the Shadow Queen may return. Azmina, if we don't act fast, your first trip to the Magic Forest might be your last."

Azmina gasped in horror. "We have to stop them!"

"Absolutely!" agreed Willa.

"No way are we letting those sprites wreck the Magic Forest," declared Naomi.

"I am very happy to hear that," said the Tree Queen.

Her branches began to wave and her leaves

rustled, as if blown by a strong wind. Azmina watched her, not sure what was going on. Finally, the queen's movements slowed and she held out one of her long arms. Dangling there was a huge, shiny golden apple.

"Look into the magic apple, Dragon Girls," she instructed.

Azmina, Willa, and Naomi leaned forward, peering at the giant apple. At first Azmina could see nothing but their own dragon-y faces in the apple's shiny surface. But slowly, shapes began to form. It was like looking into a crystal ball.

The Magic Forest came into view. Azmina saw ancient trees, glittering lakes, fields of mysterious flowers. Everything was bathed in golden sunshine.

But then she noticed something strange. It was all fading to a dull gray, like someone was turning down the color! In horror, she watched as the trees and flowers began to wither.

Azmina looked at the others with alarm.

"This must be the Shadow Sprites at work!" said Naomi.

"It's like they're stealing the sunshine," said Willa, her wide eyes fixed on the magic apple.

The Tree Queen nodded wisely. "Sunlight, moonlight—they want to take all happiness, and every shade of color. They want to make the forest a place of endless grayness. Then they will have more power. I fear they won't stop until every last glittering thing is gone and the Shadow Queen can rule again."

Azmina gave her wings a little flap and was relieved to see golden glitter swirl into the air.

The Tree Queen smiled. "Don't worry, Azmina.

Here in the glade we're safe. My magic force field is too strong for the Shadow Sprites. For now, at least. But the Magic Forest is huge, and my powers only stretch so far." The Tree Queen's branches swayed. "I cannot battle the Shadow Sprites alone."

"I'll help you!" The words burst out of Azmina. "And I bet Willa and Naomi will, too."

Willa and Naomi nodded and gave her big smiles. "Of course we will," said Willa. "We're a team. The Glitter Dragon Girl team."

A warm glow spread through Azmina. It felt good to be part of a team.

"Thank you, Dragon Girls," said the Tree Queen, her wise face serious. "But I must warn you. This quest will be dangerous. And you three don't know one another very well yet. Will you be able to work together?"

Azmina hesitated. Willa and Naomi were already friends. They were sure to work well together. But would she fit in? Azmina met first Willa's eyes, and then Naomi's. Were they thinking the same thing?

Naomi's expression immediately broke into a smile, and Azmina smiled back, feeling a surge of confidence. "We can do this."

The queen nodded, her eyes sparkling. "I believe you can."

"Azmina, pluck the apple from my branch," said the Tree Queen. Azmina did as she was told. At the top of the apple was a single leaf. "Twist the leaf," the Tree Queen instructed.

It was tricky to do this with claws, but Azmina managed it in the end. Instantly, the apple opened into two perfect halves. The inside was hollow and shiny like a golden bowl.

"There is an ancient potion that will stop the Shadow Sprites from stealing the sunshine," explained the Tree Queen. "As you collect the ingredients, place them into this magic apple. But take heed, Dragon Girls! The ingredients are powerful, and very difficult to find."

"Umm, has anyone noticed that it's getting darker and colder?" said Naomi suddenly.

"You're right!" said Azmina, looking around. The sky was definitely grayer. "Is night falling already?"

"No. It's the work of the Shadow Sprites. Look at the apple," said the Tree Queen.

Azmina joined the two halves of the apple and an image reappeared. This time it was of the Magic Forest's golden sun. But something was wrong! A sliver of the sun was not shining.

"That can't be good," muttered Naomi.

"Unfortunately, you're correct," said the Tree

Queen. "If you don't find the ingredients for the potion in time, I am afraid the sun may never shine again."

The Dragon Girls stared at her in horror.

"We won't let that happen!" said Azmina fiercely. She'd only just discovered the Magic Forest. There was no way she was going to let it be taken away from her so soon!

"You'll have to be careful," warned the Tree Queen. "The Shadow Sprites are tricky. They will do anything they can to stop you."

Just then, Azmina thought she saw something move on the other side of the force field. Was it a shape, slipping through the trees? But when she looked again, there was nothing there.

A breeze had started to blow in the forest. Trees brushed against the force field like branches on a window.

"There is not a moment to lose, Dragon Girls!" urged the Tree Queen. "The sooner you get the ingredients, the sooner the potion can be made."

The queen's leaves rustled and Azmina saw something lift, whirl through the air, and land at her feet. Azmina bent to pick it up. It was a kind of bag, made of a strange material that felt both soft and sturdy.

"This is for you to carry the apple in, Azmina," explained the Tree Queen.

Willa and Naomi helped her strap the bag

over one shoulder and around her body. The bag sat flat against her chest, blending in per-fectly with the golden tones of her glittery skin. And when she put the apple in, it barely made a bulge. Clearly, this was a very special bag!

Azmina flapped her wings, sending glitter dancing through the air. She couldn't wait to head off. Sure, it was a bit scary, especially with the Shadow Sprites lurking around. But it was exciting, too.

"What are the ingredients?" Azmina asked eagerly.

"You need to collect three things, so listen closely," replied the Tree Queen. The Dragon Girls leaned in to better hear the Tree Queen's whispery voice. "First, you need golden sunflower seeds from the Secret Valley. You must grind them into a powder."

Azmina nodded. Sunflower seeds didn't sound difficult to collect. This potion would be a cinch!

"The second ingredient is honey from the glow bees of Orb City," continued the queen.

Azmina felt a little less confident about this ingredient. Glow bees? Orb City? She had no idea what those things even meant! But she figured Willa and Naomi would know.

Outside the glade, the breeze had turned into a strong wind.

"The final and most difficult ingredient," said

the Tree Queen above the noise of the wind, "is a—"

But the wind whipped against the glade's force field, drowning out the rest of the queen's sentence.

Azmina thought she heard the word *spark* but she wasn't completely sure. "Excuse me, did you say ..."

But it was too late. The Tree Queen had already begun transforming back into her tree form. Her dress, her face, her strong brown arms had soon all turned back into solid wood.

Azmina turned to the others. "Did you hear that last thing? It was 'spark,' right?"

Willa shrugged. "Sorry. I totally missed it."

"I'm pretty sure she said 'bark,'" declared Naomi. "Yesterday when we were practicing flying, I saw a super sparkly tree. I bet we need to collect some bark from it."

"I really heard 'spark,'" said Azmina.

Naomi scrunched up her snout. "Hmm. I'm positive I heard 'bark.'"

Willa flapped her wings a little and rose up off the ground. "Let's not worry about it now," she said. "The first ingredient was sunflower seeds from the Secret Valley, right?" Azmina and Naomi nodded. "Well, let's go there, then."

"Do you know the way?" asked Azmina.

Naomi and Willa shook their heads.

Just then, Azmina felt a gentle pressure at

her neck. "Buttercub!" she cried, snuggling into him. "Where did you come from?"

"I'll always appear when you need me. Let's go," he said in his warm, purring voice.

The golden cub flapped his butterfly wings and soared into the air.

Azmina had no time to worry about her flying skills. She had to stay close behind! "Come on!" she roared to Willa and Naomi down below.

"This little guy is leading the way!"

They flew up and over the treetops. It

was amazing! In fact, it was so much fun that Azmina almost forgot they were on an important quest. Almost, but not quite. The farther they flew, the more the sunlight faded. But this wasn't the beautiful dimming of a sunset. This was something much stranger and more terrible.

Azmina clenched her jaw. She was NOT going to let the Shadow Sprites steal all the sunlight and moonlight. This place was too glittering and wonderful!

5

Flying was fun, but it was also hard work, especially as they were heading directly into the wind. All the same, as she got more and more confident, Azmina couldn't resist trying out some of the midair moves she'd seen Buttercub doing.

"Cool!" said Naomi, flying up beside her. "Hey, try this!"

Naomi then did a series of very slick moves. She swooped to the left, then quickly flipped back to the right. Then she showed the others how to flip over and fly facing up to the sky. It wasn't as easy as it looked! Finally Naomi did a very fast, downward torpedo roll.

Willa and Azmina tried to follow along. And they did pretty well...right until the final bit, when their tails nearly got tangled!

"We need to work on that one!" Azmina chuckled as they flew back up to Naomi.

"Fine by me!" Willa grinned. "Flying is one thing I'll never get sick of practicing."

Just then, Naomi gave a shout. "Look!"

Below was a field of sunflowers, hidden
between two tall mountains topped with snow
that was ever so slightly purple. The sunflowers
looked like ones Azmina had seen back in the
normal world, except for one important

difference. Their centers shone brightly, as if lit from within. Strangely, the delicious smell of fresh buttered popcorn wafted up from the field.

"Time to land!" called Azmina as Buttercub began to swoop toward the flowers. Azmina flew after him at top speed.

"These flowers are so cool!" cried Willa, landing nearby.

She was right. Now that they'd landed, Azmina saw that the seeds in the center of each bloom looked like little golden light bulbs! But not all of them seemed to be working properly. Some were flickering on and off. Others had lost their brightness.

Azmina's stomach did a weird loop. Were the Shadow Sprites somewhere nearby, stealing the light from these flowers? She glanced around. She couldn't see anything, but she had an eerie feeling the sprites were close by, watching.

Clearly, there was no time to lose. Azmina wrapped a paw around the stem of the brightest flower she could see and gave it a gentle shake.

Seeds tumbled out from the flower and scattered on the ground. As Willa and Naomi hurried over, Azmina picked one up. It felt warm and smooth.

"The Tree Queen said we need to grind them into a powder," Azmina remembered. "How, I wonder?"

"Maybe we stomp on them?" suggested Willa.

Azmina grinned as she jumped up and down on the seeds. To her surprise, the seeds crumbled to fine powder. She had always been pretty strong, but now she was dragon strong!

She pulled the apple out from her bag and twisted the top leaf around. Magically, the apple separated into two, and Azmina carefully sprinkled the glittering sunflower seed powder inside. The powder fizzed slightly as it settled in the bottom, sending up a tiny, sweet-smelling puff of steam.

The three Dragon Girls grinned at one another.

"That wasn't too hard!" said Naomi.

"Way easier than I expected," agreed Willa. "Do you think the next two ingredients will be as easy?"

Buttercub rose into the air, clearly eager to get going.

"There's only one way to find out!" said Azmina. "Come on. Let's go!"

The more Azmina flew, the faster and more agile she got. She longed to practice some of the moves Naomi had shown her, but she knew they had to stay focused on their quest. She flapped her powerful wings and felt the air glide across her glimmering body. She felt strong and sure. She and the other Glitter Dragons would fix this problem, she just knew it.

Buttercub flew higher and higher, and the others followed until the forest looked like a mossy green carpet far below.

"Isn't it beautiful?" called Willa, flying up beside her.

Azmina nodded, golden glitter spiraling out behind her.

"It is beautiful," agreed Naomi, joining them. "But have you noticed how much darker it is now?"

Naomi was right. It felt like night had started to fall.

Up ahead, Buttercub began to descend, leading the Dragon Girls back down toward the treetops. As they got lower, Azmina noticed a strange light coming from between the trees. What could it be?

Then she spotted the source of the light.

Brightly glowing spheres hung from branches all around them. "Are those things lanterns?" she wondered out loud.

"They're beehives!" exclaimed Willa.

Little bright dots flew in and around the beehives, like tiny twinkle lights.

"But bees don't shine like that," mused Naomi. "They must be fireflies."

Then all three Dragon Girls realized what they were. "Glow bees!" they cried in unison.

Azmina grinned. The second ingredient was glow honey. It looked like collecting glow honey was going to be just as easy as getting the sunflower seeds!

Together, they swooped down toward the orbs. But as they got closer, Buttercub spoke. "Careful," he said softly. "Glow bees are very touchy. You can't just rush up to them."

The Dragon Girls stopped, hovering in mid-air. Azmina could hear the glow bees buzzing. They sounded louder than normal bees, and a little bit electric, too.

"Maybe one of us should go and ask them politely for some honey?" Azmina suggested.

They all looked at one another. "You should do it, Azmina," said Willa.

Naomi nodded. "I agree."

"Me? Why me?" spluttered Azmina, surprised.

"Because you're friendly and funny and good at talking," said Willa. "I would have no idea what to say."

"Well, okay," Azmina said.

It was nice that the others thought she'd be good at talking to the bees. She wasn't so sure herself, though!

Willa smiled. "Don't worry. We'll stay close by."

Azmina nodded, hoping she looked braver than she felt. The three Dragon Girls flew closer to the orbs, being careful not to brush against any of the bees with their wings. The last thing they needed was to make them angry. Azmina gulped. The bees looked a lot bigger up close!

6

At first the glow bees just ignored Azmina, flying around her as if she were nothing more than a weirdly-shaped golden flying tree. She coughed some glittery sparks to try to get their attention, and one of the bees stopped mid-flight.

"Do you mind not doing that? It's very dis-tracting!" it buzzed irritably.

"Sorry," said Azmina politely. "We were just wondering if you could do something for us. We'd bee so grateful."

Another bee stopped. "Glow bees don't do favors!"

"And we hate bee jokes!" said the first bee.

"But if you don't help us, the whole forest could lose its sparkle!" called Naomi from where she was hovering.

"Shhh!" whispered Willa.

Naomi made a sorry face and shrugged.

"I'm sorry about the bee joke. It's just, this is

really important," said Azmina hastily. "Could we possibly talk to your queen?"

Now a whole group of bees flew up, buzzing angrily. "Glow bees do NOT have a queen! We have a democratically elected president. You clearly know nothing about us!"

Oh boy! This is NOT going well, thought Azmina. But she needed to make this work somehow. "You make the best honey in the Magic Forest," Azmina said, using her *Can I have another scoop of ice-cream?* voice. It sometimes worked on her mom. The bees buzzed again, but in a proud kind of way. "And only your special honey can help the Magic Forest right now," Azmina added quickly.

"Help? What kind of help does it need?" asked a new bee. The other bees parted to let her through. "I'm President Bee. What exactly is the problem?"

"Well, have you noticed that the sun isn't shining brightly today?" asked Azmina.

There was a buzz of agreement. "All the flowers have already started to close, but it isn't even late afternoon!" called one bee.

"It's because of the Shadow Sprites," Naomi cried.

The buzzing grew loud and angry again.

"Don't worry!" Azmina said. "We are working on a special potion to stop them. We already have one ingredient. But now we need some of your special glow honey."

She smiled at the bees. Surely they would agree. If there were no sunshine, there would be no flowers. And if there were no flowers, there would be no honey!

The bees' buzzing grew so loud that little sparks of light shot into the air.

"Absolutely not," cried one bee.

"Glow bees do NOT give away their honey,"

buzzed another. "We work very hard to make it. Why should we let you have it for nothing?"

"But we're trying to help the forest!" erupted Naomi. "You bees are—"

"Making a good point!" interrupted Azmina before Naomi could finish. The glow bees had long, gleaming stingers. She did not want to find out exactly how sharp they were!

"We don't expect you to simply give us your honey," said Azmina, thinking fast. "We could exchange it for something! Like, some glitter?" she said hopefully. "Glittery honey would be pretty amazing."

The bees went into a huddle, buzzing softly

together. The Dragon Girls exchanged nervous looks.

Finally, the huddle broke up, and President Bee flew over to Azmina. "We all agree: Our glow honey is perfect just the way it is. We don't want your glitter."

Azmina listened in dismay. What were they going to do now?

But the president hadn't finished. "However, we have another idea. We challenge you to a flying competition: bees versus Dragon Girls. We will fly through the same course. If you three can do it as well as us, we will reward you with some of our honey. What do you say?"

The Dragon Girls looked at one another. The bees had been flying all their lives. Today was Azmina's first day! It didn't seem like a fair competition. But what choice did they have?

It was clear the other Dragon Girls were thinking the same thing. Naomi shrugged, then nodded. Willa did the same.

Azmina turned back to the president. "Challenge accepted!"

Instantly, the bees began organizing themselves into rows. Within seconds they had formed into long, glowing lines. Their tiny wings flapped so fast that the air hummed like a well-oiled engine.

"This is going to be tough," muttered Willa.

"Don't worry," Azmina whispered. "At least our wings are bigger. We'll be faster, for sure."

"What exactly do we have to do?" Naomi asked President Bee.

"First, you must fly three times around each of the trees with a hive hanging from it," the bee announced.

Looking around, Azmina spotted three trees with glowing orb-hives suspended from their branches.

"But do NOT bump them or you will make the bees inside very mad," she continued.

"There are more of you?" asked Azmina.

"Oh yes," buzzed the president. "And if you disturb them, they will not be pleased. Believe me, a not-pleased bee is not pleasing to see."

Azmina swallowed. If there was something to trip over or bump into, Azmina did. Her mom joked that she even tripped over things that weren't there. *But maybe it will be different now that I'm a Dragon Girl*, Azmina thought hopefully.

"Then, once all three hive trees have been circled, you will perform a routine."

"Hang on—a what?" spluttered Naomi.

But the swarm of bees had already taken off in one graceful swoop. They circled the first tree in neat loops, then quickly moved on to

the second. By the time they finished, they were moving so fast that they looked like the glowing tail of a comet.

Next, the bees flew high above the Dragon Girls. They began to swirl to the left and to the right, up and down, tracing out beautiful glowing patterns in the air. It looked like someone was drawing pictures in the air with a sparkler.

"We are in so much trouble!" muttered Willa, which was exactly what Azmina had been thinking. "There's no way we can beat that."

7

Naomi looked stressed. "We haven't had time to practice!"

"We'll be okay," said Azmina, hoping it would be okay. "Let's do your routine, Naomi. You know, the one we did on the way here."

"The one where you and Willa got your tails

caught and nearly fell out of the sky?" said Naomi, one eyebrow arched.

"Well, yes," said Azmina. "But this time we won't get tangled. Right, Willa?"

Willa gave a nervous nod.

"It's a pretty wild plan." Naomi sighed. "But it's also the only plan we've got. So let's go for it!"

"Your turn now, dragons," buzzed the bees. "One, two, three!"

The three Dragon Girls took off, heading for the first tree. Once, twice, three times they circled it, leaving a multicolored glitter trail behind them. Because they were a lot bigger than the bees, their circles had to be bigger. The first circle was also kind of wobbly. But the second loop was perfect. On the third trip around the tree, Azmina felt her wing graze the edge of a hive.  To her relief, the hive did not move and no angry glow bees came flying out.

"We're halfway!" Azmina roared to Willa and Naomi.

"Yeah, but this is the hardest part!" Willa pointed out.

"Just do what I do, Dragon Girls!" said Naomi, swooping to the left.

Azmina and Willa copied Naomi. And they

did it perfectly! Then Naomi flipped back to the right, with Azmina and Willa doing the same. Azmina thought she could hear the bees humming in an impressed kind of way. Flying together like this was actually pretty fun. Azmina just wished they'd had time to practice the torpedo roll.

Naomi tucked in her tail and began the final move. She spun at top speed toward the ground below. Willa and Azmina exchanged a look.

"Ready . . . go!" called Willa.

Azmina was spinning so fast that she couldn't see Willa beside her, but she could sense her there.

"Wooo!" cried the bees.

And then, just as they began to slow down, everything went wrong.

"Something grabbed my paw!" cried Willa.

Azmina turned to see Willa plummeting toward the ground. Disappearing off between the trees were two thin gray shapes. Shadow Sprites!

Without thinking, Azmina swooped down after Willa. She felt someone by her side, and for a horrible moment, she thought it was another Shadow Sprite. But then she saw a burst of rainbow glitter. Naomi!

"Catch her!" roared Naomi.

With one last turbo boost of energy, Azmina managed to grab ahold of Willa's left wing. At the same moment, Naomi took hold of Willa's right one.

"Thanks, guys," said Willa, sighing, as Naomi and Azmina lowered her gently down. "I'm so sorry. I messed everything up. We'll never get the honey now."

Azmina shrugged. "The most important thing is that you're okay."

"Exactly," agreed Naomi. "Maybe there's something else we can use instead of glow honey in the potion?"

"There is no replacement for glow honey!" corrected President Bee, who was now hovering before them.

Suddenly Azmina had an idea. "Is it true that working together is the most important thing for bees?"

"Absolutely!" buzzed the president. "As we bees always say, 'The key to productivity is to always work in harmony.'"

"Teamwork is important to Dragon Girls, too," said Azmina pointedly. "Really, really important. And if one of us is in trouble, we help her out. Even if it means messing up a routine."

"Huddle!" called President Bee, and instantly

the other bees flew around her to form a big, buzzing ball.

The Dragon Girls watched nervously. What was going on?

Then the group moved apart, and President Bee approached. "We have talked about it. We agree that teamwork is everything. We will help you."

A group of bees flew right over to Azmina, holding a leaf between them. Balanced on the leaf was a drop of something not quite liquid, not quite solid. It shone like polished amber.

"It's so beautiful!" breathed Willa.

"Of course," said President Bee proudly. "Add it to your potion while it's fresh."

Azmina opened up the magic apple and poured in the honey. The sunflower seed powder instantly changed to a bubbling liquid the color of toffee. Azmina closed the apple, and the outside glowed with magic.

"Where are you going next?" asked the president.

The Dragon Girls looked at one another. It was a very good question.

"I still think we need to find some bark," said Naomi. "Follow me. I think I can remember where I saw that sparkly tree yesterday."

Azmina hesitated. "I really think the Tree Queen said spark."

"But that doesn't make sense! What even is a

'spark'?" Naomi wondered aloud. "And where would we find one?"

"Look behind you!" said the bees.

The Dragon Girls turned. Off in the distance, rising up above the trees, was a giant volcano. Shooting out from the top of the volcano were countless fiery sparks.

"That's it! That's the third ingredient!" cried Azmina.

"Would the Tree Queen really ask us to collect something from a volcano?" Naomi asked doubtfully. "That seems way too dangerous."

Azmina turned to Willa. "What do you think, Willa? Spark or bark?"

Willa looked at Azmina. Then she looked at Naomi. She swallowed. "Bark," she blurted out. "I think it was bark."

"Then let's go!" Naomi cried. "We'd better hurry. It's getting darker by the minute."

But Azmina stayed where she was. "I really think we need to collect a spark."

Glittery clouds puffed from Naomi's nostrils in frustration.

The bees watched them with interest. "Bees always agree to agree," they buzzed disapprovingly.

Azmina was worried. Would the bees try to take back their honey?

Maybe Naomi was thinking the same thing, because she shrugged and said, "Okay, you go and look for a spark. We'll go and get some bark. That way we've got double the chance of getting the right ingredient."

Azmina nodded. She was glad that Naomi wasn't annoyed with her. But as Naomi and Willa flew away, she felt utterly alone.

A gnawing feeling spread in the pit of her stomach.

Had she just made a terrible mistake?

8

Azmina turned to President Bee with a gulp. "Do you have any tips for flying to the volcano?"

"I have only one tip," buzzed the president. "Don't!"

Azmina sighed. This wasn't the advice she had been hoping for.

"The volcano has been very active recently. There are huge lava sprays. It's simply not safe," explained the president.

Azmina looked over at the volcano. Molten lava belched into the sky. There was no doubt it would be dangerous. But somehow, Azmina was sure she was meant to go there. It was almost as if the volcano was calling her.

Also, she reminded herself, *I am a Dragon Girl!* There was something about her glittering scales that made her feel extra brave.

"The burning-hot lava is not your biggest problem," said one of the bees, as if it could read her mind. "You said that the Shadow Sprites are back. If this is true, they will do anything to stop you."

"You should stick with your friends!" added another bee. "It's safer that way."

Azmina winced. She didn't want to do this on her own. But she had no choice!

Just then, she felt something soft nuzzle up against her wing. "You're not alone," purred Buttercub.

Azmina wrapped a wing around him. Going to the volcano didn't seem nearly so scary now. "Come on, Buttercub. Let's go!"

Azmina looked up as she and Buttercub flew above the treetops. The sun looked like it was being wrapped in a strange shadowy material.

So that's why it's getting darker and darker! Azmina realized. The sun was almost half covered by the material.

To make things worse, Azmina had the feeling that she and Buttercub were being followed. Every now and again she felt something cold brush against her. When she looked, there was never anything there. But the moment she turned away, the feeling would return.

"Hey, Buttercub," she said, trying to sound

cheerful and brave, "let's see how fast we can go!"

Back in her normal life, when Azmina pretended to be brave, she often ended up actually feeling brave. She just hoped it would work in the Magic Forest, too!

The volcano loomed ahead, billowing smoke and fire. Azmina frowned. Collecting a spark from a live volcano wasn't exactly something she'd done before. Things could easily go wrong!

"Don't worry," purred Buttercub in her ear. "I know you can do it."

"Thanks," said Azmina, and she meant it. She was very glad to have her little forest friend by her side.

The roar of the lava bubbling up inside the volcano grew louder and louder as they approached. Gusts of hot air swirled around them, like they were being blasted by an enormous hair dryer. A shower of sparks exploded, twinkling and glittering like falling stars.

Despite the danger, Azmina's heart leapt. She was sure now that she needed to collect a volcano spark. Azmina put her head down and began flying at full speed toward the volcano's summit. There was no way she was going to give up now!

But as Azmina and Buttercub reached the

summit, Azmina came to a sudden stop. She couldn't move forward or backward! She was trapped in some sort of net.

Azmina looked down and saw pale gray shadows wrapped around her paws and tail. The shadows were thin and almost see-through, but strong. No matter how hard she strained, she couldn't move!

"I'm caught, too!" growled Buttercub from nearby. "It's the Shadow Sprites. They've caught us in their shadow nets."

The more Azmina struggled, the tighter the net closed around her. She felt a flash of panic. "Buttercub, what are we going to do?"

The little cub gave a sad moan. He was completely covered in shadow nets.

A powerful rage gripped Azmina, pushing away her panic. *How dare they!*

A roar began to build inside her. It was bigger and stronger than anything she'd felt before. *Roooaaaar!!!*

With the sound of her roar, the shadow nets dissolved into ash. Suddenly free, Azmina and Buttercub whooshed into the air. Golden glitter streamed from Azmina's wings. Buttercub gave a happy little roar as he zoomed alongside her.

Together, they flew high above the volcano.

Down below, Azmina could see the hot lava bubbling like soup in a pot.

Suddenly, Azmina felt a sharp pain in her right wing. It hurt so much, she couldn't move it. Azmina flapped her other wing, but it was no good. No creature can fly with only one wing! She started tumbling over and over, down toward the lava.

"Flap harder, Azmina!" urged Buttercub.

"I can't. I have wing cramp!" cried Azmina as she plummeted lower and lower.

Just before she hit the boiling lava, she flapped her good wing and swung to the side of the volcano. Yes! She just managed to hook a claw over a rocky ledge to one side. She had stopped falling, but she was far from safe. She was hanging by one claw, the lava bubbling just below her!

Buttercub swooped down to the ledge, his

cute, furry face peering at her anxiously. "What should I do?"

Azmina racked her brain. There had to be a way to solve this problem! Should she send Buttercub off to tell the Tree Queen? Or maybe he could go ask the bees to help? The problem was, Azmina didn't know how much longer she could hang on!

Perhaps if I just let go, my wing cramp will disappear and I'll be able to fly to safety? she thought. But it was too risky. If her wing was still cramped, she would fall into the lava.

Azmina was fast running out of options.

She looked around and saw another rocky ledge, just above. Azmina thought that maybe she could swing herself up and onto it. It was wider and a lot more stable than where she was right now. And from there, she might be able to climb up and over the edge of the volcano.

It was a long shot, but it was the only idea she had. "Watch out, Buttercub!" she called. "I'm going to try something."

She began to count in her head. *One, two—*

But before she reached three, a shadow fell across her. Oh no! The Shadow Sprites were back! Just what she didn't need right now. Would she be able to roar them off again?

Azmina drew in her breath, preparing to release another roar. But as she tilted her head back, she stopped. For the creatures up above her weren't Shadow Sprites at all. Instead, coming closer and closer were two dragons: one silver and one rainbow!

9

"Willa? Naomi? Is that really you?" Azmina called, hardly daring to believe it.

"Yes, it's really us!" called Willa as she and Naomi swooped lower. Together, they lifted Azmina up under their own wings and carried her to the outside edge of the volcano. Fiery sparks flew over their heads like shooting stars.

"How did you know I needed help?" asked Azmina as Buttercub flew over and snuggled into her.

"We didn't," said Willa. "But leaving you didn't feel right. I mean, I know we all have to do things alone sometimes, but it felt wrong somehow."

"And I realized you were right about the final ingredient," continued Naomi. "So we turned around. But we didn't expect you to be dangling inside the volcano!"

"That wasn't exactly the plan," admitted Azmina. "I am so glad to see you two! You guys totally saved me."

"Well, we're a team, aren't we?" said Naomi

with a grin.
"Like you said
to the glow
bees. Helping
each other
is what we're
meant to do."

A spray of bubbling lava exploded nearby. Willa leaned forward. "Have you caught any sparks yet?"

Azmina shook her head. "I don't know how to. And do we need one spark, or lots of them? And how do I add it to the potion without burning myself?"

She didn't add her biggest worry. *What if*

I am wrong about spark being the last
ingredient?

"Catching a spark will be easy," Naomi said. "Just open up the apple and let it fall in."

Azmina couldn't help laughing. It was so simple, and so perfect! "Why didn't I think of that?"

"That's what friends are for, right?" Naomi grinned.

Azmina felt a warm glow as she pulled the apple from her bag. It wasn't just because of the nearby volcano. Naomi had called them friends.

"I think you'll know which spark to catch

when you see it, Azmina," said Willa in her thoughtful way. "Trust yourself."

"But you'd better do it soon," said Naomi, pointing up. "Look."

The sun was almost completely covered by the shadow cloth! There was no time to lose. Azmina grabbed the magic apple and turned to face the volcano.

When the next shower of sparks erupted into the air, Azmina found herself watching a single spark, bigger and brighter than all the rest.

"It's that one," she declared. That was her spark, for sure. Quickly, she opened the apple.

But just as the spark was almost within reach, the wind whipped it away.

"GO, AZMINA!" yelled Willa. "Catch it!"

But where had the spark gone? The air was filled with ash, making it hard to see. Then Azmina spotted something shimmering

brightly, just overhead. *That's it!* she thought. Flapping her one good wing as hard as she could, Azmina leapt into the air. She scooped up the spark with the apple and trapped it inside with the lid as she landed back on the ground.

Willa and Naomi rushed over. "Did you get it?" asked Naomi.

"I think so," said Azmina, still breathing heavily.

"Look!" said Willa, pointing to the apple.

Glittering steam was wafting out from under the lid. The Dragon Girls looked at one another. Was this a good sign, or had they just wrecked the potion?

"Open it up," urged Naomi.

Carefully, Azmina undid the lid and peered inside. The golden mixture was fizzing like soda.

"It smells so good!" murmured Willa, closing her eyes and breathing in deeply.

"But nothing's happening," Azmina cried, looking up.

The sun was still covered in shadow bandages and the forest was getting gloomier by the second.

"The potion has to be right," insisted Naomi, taking a deep breath. "It smells too good to be wrong."

Azmina agreed. Maybe they had to figure

out what to do with the potion? She closed her eyes and breathed in the aroma again. Instantly, the cramp in her wing disappeared. In fact, she felt stronger than ever.

"Um ... guys?" she heard Naomi say, an excited quiver in her voice. "Try flapping your wings. I feel really strong. It's like we've been turbo-boosted!"

Azmina opened her eyes and gave her wings a gentle flap. She shot up into the air. Naomi was right! Azmina leaned over the apple and breathed in more of the delicious smell. Then she gave two more quick flaps and sped up like a rocket, golden glitter streaming behind her.

"I get it!" cried Willa, flying up beside her. "The potion made us extra powerful. It's so we can make it all the way to the sun. Then we can rip off the bandages."

"I don't think it's possible to fly all that way," said Azmina. "And wouldn't we burn ourselves?"

"But the sun here is different," Willa pointed out.

This was true. The sun above the Magic Forest looked bigger than the one at home. It also had a purple hue. But still, it was very far away.

Azmina looked at Naomi. "What do you think?"

"Well, we have to do something," said Naomi. But she looked unsure.

Azmina nodded as she thought of the glow bees. It was more important than ever that they work together. "Let's go, Dragon Girls!" she yelled.

Together, the three Dragon Girls blasted into the air, their glitter trails streaking behind them.

Faster and higher they flew, until the volcano was a mere dot below them. But even with their new turbo-boosted flying skills, it was soon clear there was no way they could reach the sun. It was just too far away.

Azmina looked up anxiously. Only one small,

bright sliver of sun still shone. Her chest pounded with frustration. The thought of the sun being smothered was terrible! A moment later, the final golden strip of light vanished and a thick shadow fell across the land.

The shadow was so thick, the Dragon Girls couldn't even see one another's faces. Only their glittery eyes were still visible.

"We're too late!" Willa cried.

Fury built up inside Azmina. This just couldn't happen! The Magic Forest was already a part of her. The idea that the Shadow Sprites would control it was too horrible! She couldn't accept it!

"NO!" roared Azmina, louder than she had ever roared before.

"Roar again, Azmina!" called Naomi, through the shadows.

Azmina didn't understand, but she did what Naomi asked. Roaring was exactly what she felt like doing anyway. *Roarrrr!*

This time, she saw why Naomi had said that. For as she roared, the shadowy wrappings on the sun began to dissolve!

"Look!" yelled Naomi.

A single ray of sunlight—bright and warm and full of hope—had pierced the sky.

"The potion didn't just turbo-boost our wings," exclaimed Willa. "It's given us extra roar power!"

"Yes! Maybe the only thing missing from the potion is us!" cried Azmina.

"Less talking, more roaring!" Naomi laughed, a determined gleam in her eyes. "Let's blast away those shadows!"

Together, the three Glitter Dragons breathed in deeply. And then, in unison, they roared as loudly as they could. The air filled with glitter. Gold, silver, and rainbow flecks spun and tumbled over one another. This time, with the power of three roars at work, things happened much more quickly.

The shadow bindings began to fizz and fall away. A fine dust floated in the air. Gray shapes flitted around frantically, but the Shadow Sprites couldn't restore their net. As all of the dragons' colorful glitter swirled around the sun, the last of the shadowy bindings simply

crumbled into nothing.

It was the most beautiful sight Azmina had

ever seen. The sun's radiant warmth once more

filled the air. It felt so good to be there,

working alongside the other Glitter Dragons to save the Magic Forest.

"It worked!" Willa whooped. "We did it!"

Naomi hovered, a funny look on her face. "I don't know if I should laugh or cry."

"I know what I feel like doing." Azmina grinned.

She zoomed high into the air and started doing midair somersaults—one after the other. Willa and Naomi joined in. Anyone who happened to look up at that moment would have seen a very strange sight: three giggling, glittery dragons somersaulting and roaring like they'd never stop.

When Azmina was starting to feel very dizzy, Buttercub purred in her ear. "The Tree Queen sent a message via the birds. She wants to see you all."

"Then let's go!" said Azmina.

She, Willa, and Naomi each did one last

somersault before zooming down through the treetops.

Now that the sunshine was back to full strength, the forest looked even more lovely. Dappled light filtered through shining leaves. The grass and flowers seemed brighter than ever. Azmina felt the sun's gentle warmth on her back as she and the others swooped toward the glade.

Best of all, the terrible feeling that the Shadow Sprites were lurking had faded. Faded, but not disappeared completely. Azmina was pretty sure that the troublesome sprites were not going to give up so easily.

"There's the glade!" called Naomi, and together

they swooped down toward the heart of the Magic Forest, where the sunlight seemed brightest of all. As they came in to land and stepped through the shimmering air, the birds burst into song. What a welcoming party! Azmina thought her heart might burst with pride.

The Tree Queen swirled into human form, smiling warmly. "Well done, Glitter Dragons! You were given a challenge that many would have found overwhelming. You succeeded brilliantly."

"We almost messed up. A few times, actually," admitted Azmina.

The Tree Queen smiled gently. "Yes, but you always figured it out in the end. You have the makings of a truly fantastic team. Those glow bees would be proud."

Azmina, Willa, and Naomi grinned at one another. Being praised by the Tree Queen felt very, very good.

"Here's the magic apple," said Azmina,

pulling it out of her bag. But the fruit was now withered, like a forgotten apple at the bottom of a school bag. "Sorry," she said, gulping. "I don't know how that happened. It was fine before."

"Don't worry," the Tree Queen reassured her. "The apple has served its purpose. This just means this part of the quest is complete."

As she spoke, the apple gave a little shudder and with a loud pop, disappeared into a cloud of sparkling dust. The dust made Azmina sneeze seven times in a row! Willa and Naomi couldn't stop laughing. Even the Tree Queen was chuckling by the end of Azmina's sneezing fit.

Once everyone had calmed down, the Tree

Queen addressed the Dragon Girls once more. "I am proud of you, Glitter Dragons," she said. "It is difficult for a new team to find its feet— or its claws—but you are well on the way. Now you must return to your homes and rest. You'll be missed if you stay here any longer. But I need you back tomorrow. There are even bigger challenges ahead. Can I count on you all to return?"

"Of course!" they chorused.

"But how do we get home?" Azmina asked, suddenly eager to see her mom again.

"You return the same way you came," said the queen. "Choose a travel charm from something nearby to focus on, then say the chant."

A golden leaf twirled down through the air and landed in front of Azmina. She picked it up, noticing that Willa and Naomi were also holding objects, although she couldn't see what they were.

Azmina clasped the leaf, focusing on its beautiful color and the soft, cool feel of it.

Just before she began to chant, she heard

Naomi say, "Azmina, let's meet up at lunchtime tomorrow? To talk Dragon Girl business?"

Azmina grinned and nodded, too

pleased even to speak. She wasn't the new girl anymore. Now she truly belonged!

Azmina, along with the other two Glitter Dragons, began to chant:

Magic Forest, Magic Forest, come explore.
Magic Forest, Magic Forest, hear my roar!

A warm wind whipped around her, lifting her up, turning her once, then placing her down on the ground. When Azmina opened her eyes, she was back in her yard. She looked down. Her wings and paws were gone. Her golden dragon body was gone. She looked like a normal girl again.

She blinked. What had just happened in the forest already felt unreal.

The back door opened and she heard her mom calling, "Azmina! Dinner!"

But it was real, Azmina told herself as she leapt up the stairs and raced inside. *And I really am the Gold Glitter Dragon!*

Turn the page for a special sneak

peek of Willa's adventure!

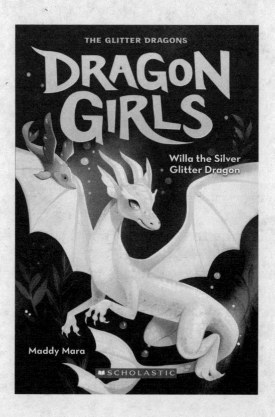

Willa couldn't help noticing that the queen looked a little tired. Were her arms thinner than usual? And her big brown eyes weren't quite so sparkly.

"Excuse me, Tree Queen, are you feeling okay?" she asked anxiously.

The Tree Queen smiled at Willa, but her smile was not as wide and bright as usual. "I am feeling better now that my Glitter Dragons are here," she said. "But it is true that I am not as strong as usual. The Shadow Sprites are still at work, you see."

"I thought we were safe in the glade." Naomi frowned.

"Everything within the glade is safe,"

confirmed the Tree Queen, "but my roots go deep into the earth and draw water from an underground river. And the Shadow Sprites are attacking the water."

Willa thought about the strange inky swirls she'd seen in the river and shuddered. She remembered what Delphina had said. "Is it true that they work for the Shadow Queen?"

The others looked at her curiously, but the Tree Queen just nodded. "She has been quiet for a very long time. But she is gathering strength."

Willa, Azmina, and Naomi exchanged worried looks.

ABOUT THE AUTHORS

Maddy Mara is the pen name of Australian creative duo Hilary Rogers and Meredith Badger. Hilary and Meredith have been collaborating on books for children for nearly two decades.

Hilary is an author and former publishing director, who has created several series that have sold into the millions. Meredith is the author of countless books for kids and young adults, and also teaches English as a foreign language to children.

The Dragon Girls is their first time co-writing under the name Maddy Mara, the melding of their respective daughters' names.